LUTON LIBR

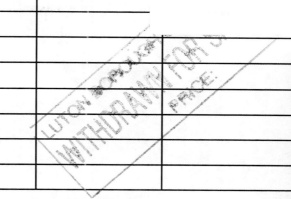

Renewals, online accounts, catalogue searches,
eBooks and other online services:

www.lutonlibraries.co.uk

Renewals: 01582 547413

Luton
Culture

Written by Chris Callaghan

Illustrated by Amit Tayal

Shinoy and the Chaos Crew

When Shinoy downloads the Chaos Crew app on his phone, a glitch in the system gives him the power to summon his TV heroes into his world.

With the team on board, Shinoy can figure out what dastardly plans the red-eyed S.N.A.I.R., a Super Nasty Artificial Intelligent Robot, has come up with, and save the day.

1 The challenge

"Why did we get lumbered with this?" asked Toby.

"Because we did a good job with the last display," said Shinoy.

"But it's lunchtime and I'm hungry!"

"Exactly!" said Shinoy with a grin. He peeked into the school office. It was empty. So was the reception area. Grabbing his rucksack, he pulled out some sandwiches and chucked one to Toby. He stretched out on the visitor sofas and pointed a remote control at the big screen display.

"Let's see if we can get the sci-fi channel!"

A burst of static on the screen revealed the Chaos Crew's enemy, S.N.A.I.R.

That was quick, thought Shinoy. He'd only pressed a few random buttons.

"Ha, ha, haaa!" laughed S.N.A.I.R. "You don't have time for rest, young fools. I have one of your precious Chaos Creeps imprisoned."

"I don't remember this one," commented Shinoy.

"Is this the one," wondered Toby, "where S.N.A.I.R. ends up in a lake of mutant monster puke?"

"No, it is not!" screamed S.N.A.I.R. "And that never happened!"

Shinoy and Toby gaped at each other. Was S.N.A.I.R. talking to them?

"The creature with wings is trapped in a temporal prison that I've created in a book. She's confined on page 67. You have until the cease of nutritional gluttony."

Shinoy and Toby pulled puzzled faces.

S.N.A.I.R. sighed. "You have until the end of lunchtime. Otherwise your flying member of the Clumsy Crew will be trapped FOREVER!"

Ember? Trapped? "But, page 67 of which book?" asked Shinoy.

S.N.A.I.R. faded from view, to be replaced with even scarier images of the teaching staff.

2 Challenge accepted!

"What's a temporal prison?" asked Toby.

"Series 2? They're used to hold a prisoner in a tiny space." Shinoy waved one of the plastic wrapped photos they'd been adding to the display. "It's like being laminated!"

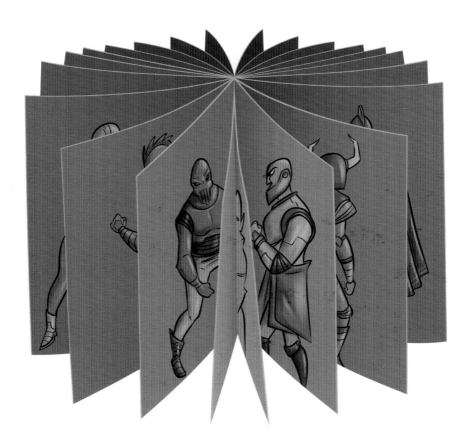

They quickly looked around for a book. But it could be any book! Anywhere!

It was definitely a reason to Call to Action, Chaos Crew! But Shinoy's phone was in his class drawer. Luckily, the big screen display was a smart screen. He found the online Chaos Crew game and tapped in his log-in details.

PORTALS OF DOOM

The screen released a flash of light and Bug stepped out.

"New delivery route," she nodded, approvingly. "I like your skills. I can't stay; Ember's missing."

"Ember's here," said Shinoy, "but we're not exactly sure where."

"She's on page 67," said Toby, trying to help.

Shinoy quickly explained.

Bug suggested she visit the computer room to use the network to detect Ember's location.

"And you two need to check as many books as you can. Double quick!"

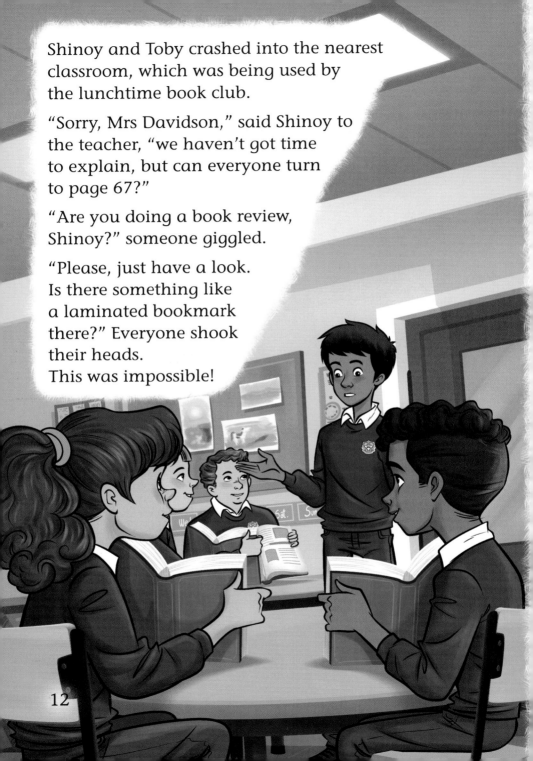

Shinoy and Toby crashed into the nearest classroom, which was being used by the lunchtime book club.

"Sorry, Mrs Davidson," said Shinoy to the teacher, "we haven't got time to explain, but can everyone turn to page 67?"

"Are you doing a book review, Shinoy?" someone giggled.

"Please, just have a look. Is there something like a laminated bookmark there?" Everyone shook their heads. This was impossible!

"Where's the best place to find books?" he wondered out loud.

"The library?" said Toby.

Of course, why hadn't they gone there first?

3 Chaos in the library

The library was empty. Not even Shinoy's mum, the school librarian, was there.

Unfortunately, there were gazillions of books. Shelves, displays and piles of them. Everywhere!

They each grabbed a book.

"This has got great pictures in it," said Toby.

Shinoy groaned. "We don't have time to browse. We need to ... oh, look, this one's about the end of chocolate!"

"Proper nightmare!"

Shinoy snapped the book shut and opened another. "Come on, no messing. We need to find Ember."

15

With a determined sense of purpose, they whooshed through page after page. Piles of books that had been checked grew everywhere like baby leaning towers of Pisa. But many more were still waiting on the shelves.

This was going to take all day.

"I've got a location!" shouted Bug, hurtling in. "It's not exact, but I know which room – the staffroom."

Shinoy and Toby stared at each other in horror and gulped, "The staffroom?"

4 Inside the staffroom

Shinoy and Toby crawled into the staffroom on their hands and knees. Pupils were not normally allowed in, but this was an emergency.

"Maybe I should help Bug," Toby whispered. Bug was fiddling with the photocopier in the corridor, just outside the staffroom.

Shinoy firmly shook his head and crawled in further. The carpet stank of stale coffee and mouldy biscuits. They couldn't see any books, just lots of teachers' feet. Ember had to be in here somewhere!

Suddenly, Shinoy's mum burst in. The look on her face told Shinoy she'd seen the mess in the library.

Shinoy stood up quickly, startling the teachers. "We're doing a library project! Can we check your books?"

"Yes," added his mum, clearly aware that something was up, "sorry to bother you."

What book would S.N.A.I.R. hide something in? wondered Shinoy. He'd put it somewhere hard to find, or in the last place they'd want to look.

"Is there a book that no one has read or ever looks at?" Shinoy asked, desperately. The staff glanced at each other.

"Well," said Miss Sharp, "there's a book written by Mr Amitri. It's called, *My Amazing Life as an Educational Expert.*"

Miss Sharp handed Shinoy the most boring-looking book he'd ever seen. He blew the dust off and looked for page 67.

A postcard-sized image of Ember was wedged between the pages. Only it wasn't an image: it was actually her, trapped in the temporal prison.

67

"Thank you!" shouted Shinoy, and he ran into the corridor.

"Now we need a blast of radiation," said Toby, banging a fist on the photocopier. "How are we going to do that?"

"Light is radiation, isn't it?" said Shinoy.

"Correct!" said Bug, jumping up from behind the photocopier, waving a spanner. "I've given it a little extra boost."

Shinoy slid the wafer-thin Ember on to the top of the copier and pressed "Scan". The display read "Warming Up". It seemed to take forEVER, until a bright beam of light whooshed across the temporal prison.

5 Freedom!

In an instant, a full-sized Ember was sitting on the copier, stretching her arms.

"Oh, that's glorious!" she smiled.

"What on *earth* is going on?" bellowed Mr Amitri.

"Just some authors visiting my library," said Shinoy's mum.

"Well, I don't care how famous you think you are," said the head teacher. "I'm not letting anyone photocopy their bottom in my school."

He suddenly noticed the book in Shinoy's hand and smiled. "I suppose you'd like me to sign that for you?"

"Yeah, that's right. That's what we're waiting for."

Mr Amitri scribbled an overly dramatic signature on the title page and swaggered away, trying not to look too pleased with himself.

My amazing life as an Educational Expert

"I'm off," said Ember. "Thanks for getting me out of that squishy nightmare." She nodded at Bug and in a flash, they were gone.

"Right then, you two," said Shinoy's mum, "you've got a lot of tidying to do in the library!"

"I could donate this to your library," said Shinoy, holding up the signed copy.

"Perfect! It's just what I need for this wobbly bookcase."

Book poetry

Bug, **Shinoy** and **Toby** crashed through the building, tripped off their skateboards **and** landed in the back of a boat!

Suddenly, a siren sounded followed by flashing lights. "Hide!" said **Bug** as two people in bright orange jumpsuits bounded on to the boat. The engines revved, and they hurtled down the platform and crashed into the waves.

They **searched** for something to hold on to as the boat bounced over the waves at top speed. Suddenly one of the people in orange turned and saw them. "What are **all** you lot doing here?" he shouted.

"No time for them, Barry, we've got a boat to find. And look, **the** nav system's gone down. Check the instruction **books**."

"It has **to** be S.N.A.I.R.!" Shinoy groaned.

"Let's **find** him."

"Look!" Toby pointed at the sky. "It's **Ember**!"

There is no greater joy than educating young minds. On my amazing journey from top-scoring contestant in an adding and subtracting competition, aged eight, to my current position as esteemed head teacher at Flat Hill school, I have drawn up my dream timetable.

This revolutionary new school timetable should, in my opinion, be rolled out to *all* the schools in the nation. A new school timetable for the modern teacher.

TIME	ACTIVITY
7:30	school starts
7:30–8:00	assembly
8:00–9:00	long run
9:00–9:30	times tables test
9:30–1:00	Maths
1:00–1:15	lunch
1:15–2:15	hard Maths
2:15–3:20	advanced Maths

Maths is, of course, the key to success. It's the reason I get up in the morning and have such an amazing life as an educational expert. Turn to page 105, for example, and you will see the joy Maths brought to me when I was on holiday in West Winton.

Ideas for reading

Written by Clare Dowdall, PhD
Lecturer and Primary Literacy Consultant

Reading objectives
- to discuss their favourite words and phrases
- make inferences on the basis of what is being said and done
- predict what might happen on the basis of what has been read so far
- explain and discuss their understanding of books, poems and other material, both those that they listen to and those that they read for themselves.

Spoken language objectives
- ask relevant questions to extend their understanding and knowledge

Curriculum links: English: Writing composition - write poetry

Word count: 1276

Interest words: imprisoned, mutant monster puke, temporal prison, confined, cease of nutritional gluttony, laminated, educational expert

Resources: dictionaries, a set of story books, pencils and paper

Build a context for reading

- Look at the image on the front cover and read the title together.
- Challenge children to predict what might happen in this story, and where it might be located.
- Read the back cover blurb and ask children to develop their predictions about the story's plot further. Make a brief note of their ideas on a whiteboard.

Understand and apply reading strategies

- Read pp2–7 aloud, as a group. Ask children to choose their favourite words and phrases from S.N.A.I.R.'s vocabulary, and discuss what can be inferred about his character from the way he speaks.
- Model how to use a dictionary to find definitions for any unfamiliar vocabulary, e.g. *temporal*.
- Create a list of emotions that Shinoy and Toby might be feeling at the beginning of the story (pp3–7).